D1512563

The Curse of the

Acropolis

Athens, Greece

by Carole Marsh

Managing Editor: Sherry Moss
Senior Editor: Janice Baker
Assistant Editor: Mark Linc
Cover Design: Mark Mackey, Rightsyde Graphics
Content Design and Illustrations: Yvonne Ford

Cover Photo Credits: Toon Possemiers, © Images from Photos.com and istockphotos.com

Cover Illustrations Credits: Mark Stay, Chih-Hang Chung, Oguz Aral

*Gallopade International is introducing SAT words that kids need to know in each new book
that we publish. The SAT words are bold in the story. Look for this special logo beside each
word in the glossary. Happy Learning!*

Gallopade is proud to be a member and supporter of these educational
organizations and associations:
American Booksellers Association
American Library Association
International Reading Association
National Association for Gifted Children
The National School Supply and Equipment Association
The National Council for the Social Studies
Museum Store Association
Association of Partners for Public Lands
Association of Booksellers for Children

20 Years Ago . . .

As a mother and an author, one of the fondest periods of my life was when I decided to write mystery books for children. At this time (1979) kids were pretty much glued to the TV, something parents and teachers complained about the way they do about web surfing and blogging today.

I decided to set each mystery in a real place—a place kids could go and visit for themselves after reading the book. And I also used real children as characters. Usually a couple of my own children served as characters, and I had no trouble recruiting kids from the book's location to also be characters.

Also, I wanted all the kids—boys and girls of all ages—to participate in solving the mystery. And, I wanted kids to learn something as they read. Something about the history of the location. And I wanted the stories to be funny. That formula of real+scary+smart+fun served me well.

I love getting letters from teachers and parents who say they read the book with their class or child, then visited the historic site and saw all the places in the mystery for themselves. What's so great about that? What's great is that you and your children have an experience that bonds you together forever. Something you shared. Something you both cared about at the time. Something that crossed all age levels—a good story, a good scare, a good laugh!

20 years later,

Carole Marsh

Hey, kids! As you see—here we are ready to embark on another of our exciting Carole Marsh Mystery adventures! You know, in "real life," I keep very close tabs on Christina, Grant, and their friends when we travel. However, in the mystery books, they always seem to slip away from Papa and I so that they can try to solve the mystery on their own!

I hope you will go to www.carolemarshmysteries.com and apply to be a character in a future mystery book! Well, the *Mystery Girl* is all tuned up and ready for "take-off!"

Gotta go... Papa says so! Wonder what I've forgotten this time?

Happy "Armchair Travel" Reading,

Mimi

About the Characters

Christina, age 10: Mysterious things really do happen to her! Hobbies: soccer, Girl Scouts, anything crafty, hanging out with Mimi, and going on new adventures.

Grant, age 7: Always manages to fall off boats, back into cactuses, and find strange clues—even in real life! Hobbies: camping, baseball, computer games, math, and hanging out with Papa.

Mimi is Carole Marsh, children's book author and creator of Carole Marsh Mysteries, Around the World in 80 Mysteries, Three Amigos Mysteries, Baby's First Mysteries, and many others.

Papa is Bob Longmeyer, the author's real-life husband, who really does wear a tuxedo, cowboy boots and hat, fly an airplane, captain a boat, speak in a booming voice, and laugh a lot!

Travel around the world with Christina and Grant as they visit famous places in 80 countries, and experience the mysterious happenings that always seem to follow them!

Books in This Series

Table of Contents

1

High Flight

"ALL ABOARD! Next stop—GREECE!" Papa called in his booming voice. Grant and Christina scrambled into the back while Papa and his wife, Mimi, settled into the front seats of the *Mystery Girl*. "One last check," Papa said. "All right, I see everyone is strapped in." He pushed the airplane's throttles forward. The red and white *Mystery Girl*, Papa's twin engine airplane, sped down the runway.

"Oh! I have slipped the surly bonds of earth..." Papa roared, as the *Mystery Girl* gently lifted off.

Oh, no, Mimi thought to herself. Not the poem again. Lately, Papa liked to recite the poem, "High Flight," after every takeoff.

"Arrrghh!" Grant, Papa's seven-year-old grandson, bellowed. Mimi concealed her grin as Grant interrupted Papa. "I'm the mighty Hercules and the only thing I'm slipping out of are these chains!" he declared, as he threw out his arms and broke the imaginary bonds.

"Hey, Grant, watch where you're flinging your arms!" Christina, his ten-year-old sister, cried out. "You almost smacked me in the nose!"

"I'm sorry, Christina," Grant said. "I guess the mighty Zeus just doesn't know his own strength," he added in a deep voice.

"I thought you were Hercules!" Christina said with a puzzled look.

"Zeus, Hercules, what's the difference? It's all Greek to me," Grant said, giggling.

"Mimi can explain the difference between Zeus and Hercules," said Christina. "She knows just about everything there is to know about Greece, like its history, culture, buildings, food, and even its mythology."

Grant looked confused. "Who is Miss Ology, and why do we even care about her?" he asked.

"Mythology is not a person, Grant," Mimi explained. "Mythology is a branch of knowledge that deals with a myth."

"I still don't get it," Grant said, looking even more confused.

"Let me explain it this way," Mimi said. "Zeus and Hercules are characters in myths, or stories told by people long ago."

"So, Zeus and Hercules are make-believe?" asked Grant.

"Yes, to people today," replied Mimi. "However, in ancient times, Zeus, Hercules, and many other gods and demigods were worshiped by the Greeks."

Grant was beginning to understand what myths

and mythology were, but he still had questions concerning Zeus and Hercules. "So, what's the difference between Zeus and Hercules, and where do they live, according to the myth?" asked Grant.

"I can answer that one, Grant," Christina said. "Zeus was the mightiest of all the Greek gods and Hercules was his son. Hercules had superhuman strength and Zeus could throw lightning bolts. Hercules' mother was human, making Hercules a demigod. Zeus lived on the top of Mount Olympus in Greece."

"Were there other gods?" Grant asked.

"Oh, yes," Christina replied. "Some of the other Greek gods were Poseidon, god of the sea; Aphrodite, goddess of love; Apollo, god of light and music; and Hades, god of the underworld. There are more, but those are the most important in Greek mythology."

"Wow, Christina, it sounds like *you're* our resident expert on Greece!" said Mimi proudly.

"I suppose this book I'm reading on Greek mythology helps a little," Christina admitted.

"Still, that's a whole lot of information to rattle off the top of your head, missy," said Papa. He cleared his throat. "May I continue?" he asked.

"Of course," said Mimi with a smile.

Papa began reciting the poem again. "...And danced the skies on laughter-silvered wings. Sunward I've climbed, and joined the tumbling mirth of sun-split clouds..."

"You know, kids, it's not polite to interrupt. Especially when it's Papa reciting his favorite poem," Mimi said with a wink, referring to Grant's recent Hercules imitation.

Grant and Christina giggled in the back of the airplane. They knew this was Mimi's way of getting Papa to stop.

"Okay, I get it," Papa said. "Enough of the poem already."

"Well, we have heard it on every takeoff these past few months," Mimi remarked. "By my count, that makes ten times," she added, holding up both hands.

"I didn't realize you were counting," Papa said, as he began to laugh.

"Mimi, will we get to meet any kids in Greece?" Christina asked. "And if we do, are they going to be in your next mystery book?" She loved going on trips with her grandmother, an author of mystery books for children.

Mimi took off her sparkly designer sunglasses and shrugged her shoulders. "You are planning on writing a mystery set in Greece, aren't you?" Christina pleaded.

"I think Mimi wants to keep us in suspense," Papa said. "Her silence helps develop the proper mysterious mood."

"Why, Papa, you're becoming quite the sleuth!" Mimi declared. "Don't worry, Christina, you and Grant will get to meet my friend Nick Pothitos and his two grandchildren. Nick is an expert on ancient Greece. The Greek government has asked him to lead several archaeological expeditions. He's even invited all of us to accompany his team on their first dig at the Acropolis." She winked at Christina. "And, I *will* write that mystery," she added.

"Now I can rest, knowing we'll meet some kids and Mimi will write a Greek mystery," Christina said. "And I am soooo tired." She snuggled deep into her seat and drifted off to sleep.

Thump.

Thump.

Thump.

Thump.

WHACK!

Christina jumped! She had never heard that sound before. She stared out the window. "Noooooo!" she cried. "This can't be happening!"

2

She's Out of Control

The *Mystery Girl* spiraled through the sky, out of control. Christina was stuck, pinned against her seat. She could barely move a muscle. The force of the rotating airplane had them all trapped.

This must be a nightmare, she thought. I know, I'll close my eyes and when I open them again, I'll be awake. Christina closed and then reopened her horrified eyes. "This is no dream!" she shouted.

"You're right, Christina, this isn't a dream," said Grant. "It's real and even better than the biggest roller coaster I've ever ridden."

"I don't think Papa is doing this on purpose," Christina said. She could see sweat dripping from Papa's forehead.

"Wheeeee, this is fun!" screeched Grant.

"Easy, girl," Papa urged. He struggled to regain control of the *Mystery Girl*. The little plane shook as Papa brought her under control. "That's it," he said calmly. Papa was not one to panic in a crisis. The *Mystery Girl* groaned as it returned to straight and level flight.

"That was fun," Grant squealed.

"More fun than I care to have in a while," Mimi replied.

"Too much 'fun' for me," Christina agreed.

"We hit some pretty rough air," Papa explained. "The turbulence along with one of the engines acting up caused the *Mystery Girl* to run wild. I've got this bucking bronco back under control and she'll behave herself the rest of the way."

"Look at the beautiful sea below," said Mimi, as she attempted to get everyone's mind off the near calamity. Grant and Christina pressed their noses against the *Mystery Girl's* windows to get a better view.

"I've never seen such beautiful blue and turquoise colors—and *those* must be islands ahead!" exclaimed Christina. "Where are we, Papa?"

"Straight below us is the Aegean Sea," said Papa. "By my calculations, those tiny dots dead ahead are the Sporades Islands. Those islands lie just off the coast of mainland Greece."

"I didn't know that Greece has islands," said Grant.

"Greece has many islands," Mimi explained.

"Will we get to visit some of the Greek Isles?" asked Christina.

"Of course," said Mimi. "We'll also eat lots of *baklava,* my favorite Greek dessert."

"Baked lava. Yuck!" Grant said with a frown.

"No, silly. *Baklava* is a sweet pastry," Mimi said. "It's yummy and you'll love it."

"Does everybody have their seat belts fastened?" asked Papa. "Yes!" Mimi, Christina, and Grant shouted.

"*Mystery Girl*, you are cleared to land," said the Athens airport tower controller. "Roger, Athens tower, *Mystery Girl*, copies cleared to land," Papa said in his firm pilot voice. As he pulled the throttles of the *Mystery Girl* back for landing, the airplane began to vibrate. "Is it me or the airplane?" Papa mumbled.

Boing! Boing!

The *Mystery Girl* bounced down the runway.

Papa brought the little airplane to a stop just beneath the airport's tower. "Not my best landing," Papa admitted.

"Are you okay, Papa?" asked Grant. "I'm fine, little fella," Papa said. "But I sure could go for something to eat right now!" Papa looked white as a sheet. Christina and Grant glanced at each other. Christina noticed Mimi's concern. "I think Papa must be famished," said Mimi. "We'll go through Customs and then get a bite to eat."

"Grant," Christina whispered. "I had a nightmare and I'm afraid it's coming true! It had something to do with Papa, an oracle, and the Greek god Apollo."

"Don't worry about that dream because the man who put gas in the *Mystery Girl* at our last stop gave me a good luck amulet," said Grant. "Uhhhh—on second thought, maybe we should be worried about those motorcycles headed straight for us!"

A Different Kind of Chariot

"I don't like the looks of this," Christina said with a shudder. Papa's face turned crimson. "Me neither," he said with his fists clenched.

Still buckled in their seats, Christina, Grant, Mimi, and Papa gaped at the ominous sight before their eyes. Side by side, four massive motorcycles rumbled ever closer. The motorcycle riders were dressed in black from head to toe. Each of them wore a shiny leather jacket and leather pants along with boots, gloves, sunglasses, and helmets.

Christina heard a shrill cackle coming from one of the motorcycle riders. It was barely audible above the motorcycles' throaty roar. She shivered as a chill shot down her spine.

"They're going to crash right into us!" Christina screamed. At the last second, the motorcycles broke away and the sinister riders circled the *Mystery Girl* in single file.

"This is just like cowboys and Indians," Grant gleefully exclaimed, "like when all the Indians hoop, holler, and ride on horses around the covered wagon. Maybe this is how the Greek Indians dress, and that's what their Indians ride over here."

"Well, *this* cowboy is about to put a stop to their nonsense," Papa growled as he stepped out of the airplane and promptly tumbled to the ground.

Papa dusted off his neatly pressed jeans and vest and lifted himself from the concrete. Stetson hat now back in place, he looked every bit the cowboy. Papa challenged the dark riders with an outstretched hand. "STOP!" he shouted at the top of his lungs.

A Different Kind of Chariot

Instantly, the mysterious strangers came to a stop. The tallest one slowly stepped off his machine. Cautiously, he removed his sunglasses and helmet, revealing a head full of long, thick gray hair and friendly brown eyes. The man stood in front of Papa with his hands on his hips and a big smile.

"Papa, I'd like you to meet Dr. Nicholas Pothitos," Mimi said. "These are my grandkids Christina and Grant." Christina's and Grant's arms were wrapped tightly around Mimi's waist.

"Puh... puh... pleased to meet you, sir," Grant and Christina murmured in unison.

Papa jerked his head around. In all the commotion, he didn't realize that Mimi, Christina, and Grant had already climbed out of the *Mystery Girl* and stood behind him. "Everyone seems to be full of surprises today," Papa remarked. "Pleased to meet you, Dr. Pothitos."

"*Ya Soo*, and call me Nick," Dr. Pothitos said, as Papa and the archaeologist shook hands. "*Ya Soo* is Greek for hello."

"You scared us to death, Nick! All dressed in black and the four of you charging at us on those noisy motorcycles," Mimi exclaimed. "How did you get by airport security, and who are your 'partners in crime' here?"

"Well, as far as security goes, I got permission from one of my good friends who is in charge of everything that goes on at this airport," he explained. "These other three 'partners in crime,' as you call them, are members of my archaeological team. They also happen to be your transportation to the hotel today."

Mimi's jaw dropped in disbelief. "You want me to get on that thing in my high heels?" she asked.

"It sounds fun to me," Papa said.

"Can we do it, Mimi?" Grant begged. "Please, Mimi? Pretty please?"

"It does seem thrilling," Mimi confessed. She slung her red scarf around her neck. "Kids, be sure to hang on tight!"

"Riding through the streets of Athens on a Harley Davidson motorcycle..." Dr. Pothitos mused. "What better way is there to truly feel the exhilaration that is part of this great city and nation?"

"What about our luggage?" Christina asked.

"Don't worry. My people will have it waiting for you at the hotel," Dr. Pothitos replied. "It will be easier for you to make it through the airport without all your heavy bags."

Christina was exhausted from all the excitement. She was not looking forward to riding on the back of a motorcycle. Goose bumps crawled across her skin every time she thought about the dream she had aboard the *Mystery Girl*. "Grant, I've got to tell you my nightmare before it's too late," she said, grasping his arm.

"We'll meet you just outside the main terminal, Nick," Mimi shouted as the four riders raced away.

The terminal was packed with tourists waiting in line to clear customs. Mimi always hated long lines, but Christina was happy for the wait. It gave her a chance to tell Grant about the nightmare.

"Grant," Christina whispered. "Grant!" Her brother was fascinated with all the signs posted throughout the airport. He didn't notice Christina standing next to him, discreetly trying to get his attention. "It's all Greek to me," he said, attempting to make sense of the unusual Greek alphabet.

"It is confusing, Grant, but I can understand just enough Greek to help us get by," Mimi reassured him.

"Grant!" Christina whispered again. She yanked his arm.

"Careful, you shouldn't disturb the mighty Zeus," Grant said with a solemn look on his face. "You don't want me to hit you with one of my mighty lightning bolts, do you?"

"Grant, I'm serious," Christina said. "The dream had an oracle in it."

"An oracle? What's that?" Grant asked.

"Mimi says an oracle is a person who brings a message on behalf of a deity, like one of those Greek gods we were discussing," Christina explained. "In my dream, the oracle was hissing and pointing his fingers at Papa. It was dressed like Dr. Pothitos, except the oracle didn't wear a helmet or sunglasses. It then let out a bloodcurdling shriek and said Papa was cursed by the power of Apollo. I heard that exact same shrieking sound when the motorcycles were circling us."

"That's really spooky," Grant said.

"I'm not sure my dream will come true," Christina said. "It could be a warning. Maybe we shouldn't trust Dr. Pothitos."

"Yeah, I wonder about him, too," Grant agreed.

"Grant, what else can you tell me about your good luck amulet?" Christina asked. It seemed to her they'd had nothing but bad luck ever since Grant had laid his hands on it.

"The guy who gave it to me was wearing—" Grant was interrupted before he could finish.

"You kids ready to hit the trail?" Papa asked, reaching down to tousle Grant's blonde hair.

"You bet!" replied Grant and Christina.

With passports stamped, the four **resolute** travelers weaved their way through the crowded terminal. The four black-clad riders were waiting, as promised, outside. Mimi, Papa, Grant, and Christina each went to the back of a different motorcycle. Christina's stomach tightened as they sped off on the large bikes. *There was something eerie about these drivers and their motorcycles.*

A Greek Tragedy

The motorcycles raced through the winding streets. "Yipee yi oh kai yea," Papa sang out. Dr. Pothitos, with Papa holding on, was leading the pack of motorcycles dodging thick traffic through the bustling streets of Athens. Mimi and Grant, holding tight to their drivers, followed close behind. Christina and her driver brought up the rear.

With her arms firmly attached to the mysterious man in front of her, Christina turned for a better view. She gazed at the gigantic green mountains surrounding her. The huge mounds dwarfed the city's skyline. Houses and buildings stretched to the top of the mountains. Beautiful white churches with electric blue domes dotted the landscape. Now and then, she caught glimpses of the sparkling blue Aegean Sea. The contrast of the white marble buildings against the jewel-toned blue sea and emerald green mountains was breathtaking.

"How much further?" Christina shouted, her brown hair flapping against the back of her helmet. There was no response. "How much further?" she asked again. As the driver fidgeted in his seat, Christina nearly slipped off the bike. She was terrified. Was this man trying to toss her from the motorcycle? This relaxing, scenic ride had become a nightmare!

Dr. Pothitos motioned with his hand for the others to slow down. Christina was relieved that this crazy ride was nearly at an end.

Just ahead of her, Mimi's and Grant's motorcycles had stopped. As Christina's motorcycle slowed, she saw Mimi and Grant hurriedly throw their helmets aside. They leaped off their Harley Davidson motorcycles and rushed down the street. Where could

Papa be? He was just ahead of them before the last corner.

Christina strained her eyes. Way ahead, she spied Papa and Dr. Pothitos sprawled atop a stack of cardboard boxes. Christina immediately dropped her helmet and raced behind Mimi and Grant. "Papa, Papa!" she cried out.

"Are you okay, Papa?" Grant asked, concerned.

"Yes, I'm all right," Papa replied, "but we should check on our friend here. Are you okay, Nick?"

"I feel fine," Dr. Pothitos said, grunting as he stood up. "However, I think my Harley has seen better days." *Better days* was quite an understatement. The motorcycle was a wreck.

Papa, Dr. Pothitos, and two of the other motorcycle drivers dragged the mangled bike to the curb. The mysterious fourth driver, Christina's chauffeur, had disappeared.

"Our phantom driver has disappeared again, I see," Dr. Pothitos observed.

"Phantom?" Christina inquired.

"He likes to call himself that," Dr. Pothitos explained. "He claims he's a phantom because he's here, there, and everywhere at the same time. It does seem like he's everywhere all at once."

"Like a real ghost?" asked Grant.

"He's no ghost," Dr. Pothitos continued. "He's a brilliant archaeologist and is asked to speak all over the world. He is scheduled to give so many lectures in so many places that it seems like he has to be everywhere at once. That's why I call him 'The Phantom.' Earlier, he told me he had to leave right after we dropped you off at the hotel."

"Well, that explains that," Papa remarked.

"I wish I had an explanation for this," Dr. Pothitos said, looking at the pile of junk that was once his prized bike. "I just couldn't stop. Lucky for us, we fell on this pile of cardboard boxes."

"It's not your fault, Nick," Papa chuckled. "Recently, it seems everything I touch loses control. I guess now we can add everything and *everyone* to the list."

Stunned, Christina and Grant stood motionless. Could it be Papa was under a curse? If so, how could the curse be lifted? They had to find an answer.

"Why don't the four of you get checked in here at your hotel?" Dr. Pothitos suggested. "The entrance is right around the corner."

"That sounds wonderful," Mimi said. "We'll catch up with you later, Nick. Be sure to bring your grandkids. Grant and Christina can't wait to meet them."

Mimi had no idea just how anxious Grant and Christina were to meet the other children. "Christina, I wonder if Dr. Pothitos' grandkids will be able to help us figure out this oracle stuff?" asked Grant.

"I hope so," said Christina. "I need to find out about Apollo's curse."

Grant curled his arm to show off his scrawny bicep muscle. "Even if they can't help, you've got the mighty Hercules here," he said with a grin.

Papa checked into the hotel and pointed to the luggage waiting for them, just like Dr. Pothitos had said.

"Get along, little doggies," Papa said, turning to the rest of his family waiting nearby.

"Will you need any help with the luggage, sir?" asked the hotel's bellman.

"No thanks," said Papa. "I'll take it from here." He loaded the bags on the rolling luggage carrier but struggled as he pushed it throughout the hotel. The carrier seemed to control him. Exhausted from battling the pile of bags on the rolling cart, Papa patiently waited for Mimi to fish the room key out of her purse. As she opened the door to their room, the luggage and Papa tumbled to the floor.

"Just call me fumble fingers," Papa said with a sigh, sitting in the middle of the scattered luggage.

Christina and Grant dragged their bags into the adjoining room. "Papa's just not himself at all," Christina exclaimed. "He needs our help. Right, Grant? *Grant?*"

5

Video Games and Amulets

Not again, Christina thought. Grant had a way of slipping away, getting lost, or just not being in the place where you expected him to be. Christina was annoyed that she had to find Grant again.

"Grant?" Christina called. "This isn't funny anymore." He's got to be here somewhere. Christina retraced her steps. Perhaps, he went this way, she thought.

At the end of a long hallway, Christina heard the sound of children giggling. One of them sounded like Grant! She breathed a sigh of relief and peeked in the door, which was partially open. There was Grant, perched on a bed playing a video game. Two dark-haired children sat on either side of him.

"Rats, I lost again," Grant said. "I'm never gonna get past this level!"

"My turn," claimed the girl. "No, it's my turn," insisted her brother.

"Would you care to introduce me to your friends, Grant?" asked Christina.

The three kids jumped off the bed. "I'm Alex and this is my little sister Melina," the boy announced. "You must be Christina."

Alex and Melina were the grandchildren of Dr. Nicholas Pothitos. Alex was a bright, quiet, 11-year-old boy. He loved history, video games, and solving puzzles. His sister Melina, 8, was an energetic type who liked video games as well as playing with dolls.

"We noticed the two of you in the hall and I figured that you were Carole Marsh's grandkids," Alex said. "We are *totally* into her mystery books. We got Grant's attention but you kept walking down the hall."

"I was going to run back and get you, Christina," said Grant. "But I just couldn't stop playing this video game. Sorry!"

"It's okay, Grant," she said, tapping her feet. "Just don't let it happen again."

"Will we be in your *Ya Ya's* newest mystery book?' asked Melina.

"*Ya Ya?* You mean 'grandmother'?" questioned Christina.

"Yes," replied Melina. "*Ya Ya* is what I call my grandmother."

"Mimi gave me her word that you two would be in the mystery book," said Christina.

squealed Melina and Alex.

"Why are you guys here at this hotel?" Christina asked.

"We're here on vacation to help our grandpa show you around Greece," Melina said. "We live in a town way to the north of Athens called Thesoliniki. Actually, I have something for you as a welcome present," she added. She reached in her dresser and pulled out a beautiful porcelain doll dressed in a native Greek costume. "Just for you, Christina."

"It's beautiful," exclaimed Christina. "Thank you!"

Alex pulled a baseball out of his backpack. "Since I heard you love baseball, Grant, I saved this," Alex said with a smile. "I went to New York with my grandpa last summer. He took me to a New York Yankees baseball game.

I caught this foul ball, and some of the players signed it for me after the game."

"Wow!" Grant shouted. "Thanks! Wait until everyone hears that I went all the way to Greece to get a baseball from New York!"

The kids settled back down comfortably on the bed.

"Hey, what do you know about oracles, Alex?" asked Christina.

"In ancient Greece, people worshiped Zeus, Poseidon, Aphrodite, Apollo, and many other mythical gods," Alex explained. "A high priest or priestess would speak, delivering a message from the god. The messenger was called the oracle."

"That's what Mimi said, too," Christina said.

"What's a high priestess?" asked Grant.

"Someone who was in charge of the god's temple," Alex explained. "The high priest or priestess was very powerful, and people listened to them. Christina, why are you so interested in oracles?"

"One came to me in a dream," said Christina, "and the dream seems to be coming true.

According to the Oracle of Apollo, Papa is cursed. Since my dream, everything he touches seems to go wrong. If this is a curse, how do we break it?"

"To break the curse, the god usually wants you to leave a few coins and worship them at their altar," said Alex. "Christina, I wouldn't worry. It sounds like your dream is just your mind playing tricks on you. Maybe you're just remembering a scene from a scary movie or something."

"You talk like a grown up," said Grant.

"I do have an IQ of 150," bragged Alex. "I *am* a genius."

"Oh, no, here we go again," Melina said. "Alex is bragging about how smart he is."

"I'm not bragging," said Alex. "They asked something and I told them the answer."

"They didn't ask you about your IQ," Melina said, making a face at Alex.

"We don't have to worry about Christina's dream," Grant said with confidence. "I have an amulet. It brings good luck."

Maybe Grant was right. They had landed in Greece safe and sound. Papa was lucky not to be hurt in the motorcycle crash, and Christina had found Grant safe and sound in the room with her new friends.

Grant reached into his pocket and pulled out a large gold token three times the size of a quarter. Black onyx stone protruded from its center. A cryptic message lay inscribed in the gold. "It has some sort of strange letters written on it," Grant said. "It's all Greek to me."

"Can I see that?" asked Alex. Grant handed Alex the glimmering black and gold object.

"Let me see it, too," Melina said. *She began to cringe as they silently read the dreadful message.*

6

Lucky Charm— or Not!

"Grant, tell me about the person who gave you this," said Alex.

"He was the man who put gas in the *Mystery Girl*," said Grant.

"Okay," Alex said, "but I need more details."

Grant folded his arms across his chest. "As he was putting gas in the wings," he said, "I was standing around watching him. When he finished, he said, 'You kids have a long trip ahead and could probably use some luck. Take this amulet and you'll be lucky.'" Grant shrugged his shoulders.

"He seemed kind of creepy, but the amulet looked cool."

"What was creepy about him?" asked Christina.

"As he handed me the amulet, he had a funny look on his face," said Grant.

"What kind of funny look?" Alex asked.

"Sort of an evil grin," said Grant.

"What else can you tell us about him?" asked Alex.

"He was dressed all in black and wore a silver ring on his pinkie finger," said Grant. "The ring was shaped like a skull. The man downstairs who wanted to help us with our bags was wearing one just like it."

"You mean the bellman?" Christina asked.

"Yeah, that's the guy," Grant replied.

"On the pinkie finger—what an unusual place to wear a ring," said Christina.

"That's what I thought, too," said Grant.

"Is that all you can tell me, Grant?" asked Alex.

"Enough with the questions," Melina pleaded. "They want to know what it says on the amulet, and if you don't tell them, I will."

"I'm just trying to gather all the pieces of the puzzle first," said Alex. "Then we can help Christina and Grant with this mystery." Alex read the inscription that was written in Greek.

Apollo curses those who do not heed the words of my Oracle.

"We've got to tell Grandpa Pothitos about this," Melina said.

"He'd just tease us and call us silly," Alex said. "Besides, this amulet doesn't really curse anything. It's only a warning not to ignore Apollo's messenger."

Christina scratched her head in bewilderment. "Why would someone give us this amulet and then lie about its true meaning?" Christina asked.

"I wonder when and where we will hear from Apollo's Oracle," said Alex, staring at the ominous object in his hand.

Grant grabbed the amulet from Alex's hand. "I don't know why that creepy guy gave it to me," he said. "But I've got the solution to our problem."

"What is it?" asked Christina.

"You'll find out when I'm done," said Grant.

"Excuse me," said the hotel bellman, popping his head through the open door. "I was checking to see if you needed anything special from the hotel."

"No, thanks," they replied.

"That was nice of him," said Melina.

Christina didn't like the looks of the bellman and felt he was being a bit too nosy. "Grant, we'd better get back to our room now," she said. "Mimi and Papa will be worried if they come by our room and we're not there. It's been nice to meet you, Alex and Melina. Grant and I will see you later."

"Probably sooner than later," said Alex. "Grandpa mentioned he was **cordially** inviting friends from America to join us for dinner. My guess is that *you* are those friends!"

Make Mine Souvlaki

"It's all Greek to me," Grant said, turning and flipping his menu over and over again. "I can't make heads or tails of these symbols... words...whatever."

"Take it easy, son, I'm getting dizzy just watching you," said Papa.

"Dr. Pothitos and his grandkids should have been here a half hour ago," said Mimi. "I wonder what could be taking them so long."

"Maybe they got tied up in traffic," said Christina.

"Mystery solved," Papa blurted out. "That's him coming through the door and those two young ones with him must be his grandkids."

"I'm terribly sorry to keep all of you waiting," Dr. Pothitos said, apologizing. "I'd like to introduce you to my grandchildren. This is Alex, and this is Melina."

"Pleased to meet you," said Alex and Melina, giggling softly.

"Alex and Melina, these are my grandchildren, Christina and Grant," Mimi said, not knowing the kids had already bumped into one another. "I am sure you will all get to know one another quite well over the next few days."

"Pleased to meet you, too," said Christina and Grant, winking at Melina and Alex.

"After I dropped you off at the hotel, I had my mangled motorcycle delivered to my friend's repair shop," Dr. Pothitos said. "As I suspected, it was damaged beyond repair. I asked my friend to salvage what he could."

"Sorry to hear about your motorcycle, Nick," said Mimi. "You sure seemed to enjoy riding it."

Dr. Pothitos leaned forward in his chair. "I told my friend about the accident and he thought it was strange that the brakes on a bike as new as mine would suddenly stop working," he said quietly. "He thought someone might have tampered with them. He examined the motorcycle as best he could, but it was too badly damaged for him to tell for sure what the problem was." He sat back in his chair. "Enough of my problems," he added. "What is everyone hungry for?"

"I'm so hungry I could eat a horse," Papa said.

"I suggest *souvlaki,*" said Dr. Pothitos. "Or, you should consider *moussaka,* which is baked lamb with potatoes, or try grilled octopus in vinegar, oil and oregano. Really, you will enjoy all of the Greek dishes they serve here."

"You'll have to get used to Papa's expressions, Dr. Pothitos," Christina said with a giggle. "He doesn't actually want to eat a horse."

"I should hope not," said Dr. Pothitos. "At least not when there are all these Greek delicacies to choose from."

"Nick, what do you think the kids would like to eat?" Mimi asked.

"I recommend *souvlaki* for the kids, too," said Dr. Pothitos. "*Souvlaki* is grilled meat in pita bread topped with tomatoes, onions and *sadziki,* a cucumber and garlic yogurt."

With help from their Greek friends, Mimi, Papa, Christina and Grant ordered dinner. The waitress returned with several plates piled high with delicious-smelling food.

"This *souvlaki* is so good," Christina exclaimed. "I could eat it every day."

"I'm with you, Christina," said Grant. "Yummm!"

"I never thought I'd say it," Papa commented, "but this grilled octopus is delicious. It tastes just like steak. You Greeks sure know how to cook!"

"Mimi hasn't said a word," Grant remarked. "She must not like her food."

Mimi was busy trying to figure out what made her dish taste so good. "It has eggplant layered in meat sauce," she said. "I detect cinnamon, and a rich cream sauce tops it off. It's just wonderful," she continued, taking another bite.

"The master detective has correctly uncovered the riddle of the *moussaka*," Dr. Pothitos said with a grin.

"It's just a matter of finding the clues and using your brain to piece them together," Mimi said, laughing.

"I like the music they are playing," said Christina. "Alex, do musicians play at every restaurant in Greece?"

"Not every restaurant has musicians," he said. "But if there is music playing, dancing and singing are sure to follow."

The restaurant erupted into all-out celebration. The walls echoed with the sounds of Greek music, and people crying out,

"What does *'opa'* mean?" Christina asked.

"It does not really have a meaning," said Dr. Pothitos. "It is just an expression we traditionally use when dancing—a shout of joy!"

"I hope you saved room for dessert," said the waitress, clearing the empty plates from the table.

"Of course we did," declared Mimi. "Four orders of *baklava* for us!"

"Make that a total of seven orders of *baklava*," said Dr. Pothitos.

The sweet dessert made of flaky pastry layers with nuts, sugar, syrup, honey, and cloves was Mimi's favorite. "I told you it would be yummy, Grant," said Mimi, savoring every bite.

"You sure were right, Mimi," Grant said, as the *baklava* disappeared from his plate.

"I've eaten so much you kids are going to have to roll me back to the hotel," Papa said with a smile, rubbing his stomach.

"We'd better get back to the hotel before it gets too late," said Mimi. "We have a full day planned tomorrow and we'll need to get a good night's rest. We'll see you tomorrow, Nick. Bye, Alex and Melina!"

As Papa rose, he tripped over his chair and came crashing down on the table next to him. The people at the next table barely noticed. They smiled as they helped him up and continued singing.

Melina felt sure that Papa truly was cursed by Apollo. Christina and Grant were so worried for Papa they didn't notice that the waiter holding the door for them on the way out was wearing a silver ring on his pinkie finger.

"You kids be sure and get straight to sleep," said Mimi.

"We will," they promised and entered their hotel room adjoining their grandparents' room.

"What's that sticking out of your pocket, Grant?" asked Christina, as Grant hung his jacket in the closet. *The waiter holding the door had slipped Grant a note.*

The Parthenon at Sunrise

"Look at the beautiful sunrise," exclaimed Mimi, sipping her coffee. She turned her head around and gazed at the Parthenon.

"I chose this hotel for you because you get a fantastic view of the Parthenon from the café here on the rooftop," Dr. Pothitos said.

"And I sure am enjoying the breakfast **buffet** they serve here," Papa said. "There are so many choices!"

"I thought you would still be stuffed from last night, Papa," said Christina.

"I reckon octopus doesn't stick to your ribs like steak," Papa commented.

"What's an *acro-police* and a *part-unknown*?" asked Grant.

"That is a great question, Grant," Dr. Pothitos said. "Let me tell you about the Acropolis and the Parthenon."

Dr. Pothitos explained that *Acropolis* means the edge of a town or a high city. "The early settlers of Athens chose to build their city fortress on a hill with steep sides so they could better defend themselves from attack," he explained. "The hill and the buildings on top of it are called the Acropolis."

Dr. Pothitos pointed out the window. "Grant, can you see that hill with the big white building on it?" he asked.

"Yes, I see it," said Grant. "It looks close enough to touch."

"That hill and all those buildings on it are called the Acropolis," Dr. Pothitos said.

"What about the *part-unknown?*" asked Grant.

"The Parthenon is that biggest white building with the cigar-shaped columns on top of the hill," he said. "It is one of the most famous and important buildings in the world."

He told them that the Parthenon was built over 2,500 years ago. It was originally built as a temple to honor Athena, the patron goddess of Athens. The Parthenon also served as the treasury, the place where the city kept its money. Over 400 years ago, an invading Turkish army occupied it and used it as a place to store cannonballs and gunpowder.

"That's so cool," said Christina. "Can you tell us more?"

"Not now, please," said Grant. "My head is too full from all that stuff you already told us."

"When we finish breakfast, Dr. Pothitos is going to take us on a sneak preview of the new museum," said Mimi.

"It will be open for everyone to view next year," Dr. Pothitos explained. "We still have many more artifacts to move from the Acropolis and the old museum. Our new museum will eventually house countless artifacts from the Acropolis."

Mimi, Papa, and Dr. Pothitos were busy discussing Greek history and didn't realize the kids were whispering about the note Grant received the night before.

"Grant," Alex and Melina whispered, "what did the note say?"

"How do you know about the note already?" asked Christina.

"We saw the waiter at the door slip it in Grant's pocket when you left the restaurant," said Alex. "I got a close look at him, and he had a silver ring in the shape of a skull on his finger."

"On his pinkie finger?" asked Christina.

"Yes," said Melina.

"Just like the bellman and the guy who gave me the amulet," Grant added.

"So, what does it say, Grant?" Alex asked. Grant passed him the note.

BEWARE!

They will stop at nothing!

A friend, concerned for your safety.

"Why is our 'friend' wearing the suspicious ring on his pinkie?" Christina asked. "He may be trying to gain our trust now so he can trick us later. There's got to be an explanation for all this."

Mimi interrupted the kids. "We'd better get going if we're going to make it to the museum and be done with the tour by noon," said Mimi. The children followed her to the stairs.

As Papa approached the last step on his way down the staircase, he lost his footing and fell to the ground. Christina and Grant gasped. They stood motionless, wondering if there truly was a curse on Papa.

Grant pulled the amulet from his pocket. *I know just what I'm going to do with this,* he said to himself.

I'm Losing my Marbles!

"Look, Papa," Grant exclaimed. "In the sky! There's a mummy. I didn't know they could fly!"

"Well, look at that," Papa remarked. "Have you ever seen such a sight?"

High above their heads, a helicopter hovered with its strange cargo suspended beneath.

"I can explain that," Dr. Pothitos said. "We are transferring the marbles from the Acropolis to our new museum here," he added, as the group entered the museum. "The whole process should be complete in a few more months."

"So, if that wasn't a mummy, then what was it?" asked Grant, staring at all the strange-looking artifacts.

"That was just *one* of our prized marbles from the Acropolis," Dr. Pothitos explained. "It has been wrapped like a mummy to protect it during transportation. It is absolutely priceless."

"Priceless?" Grant asked. "Marbles are priceless here? Wow! I'm gonna make a fortune off these."

Grant reached in his pocket and pulled out a handful of round glass marbles. The shiny baubles slipped from his fingers.

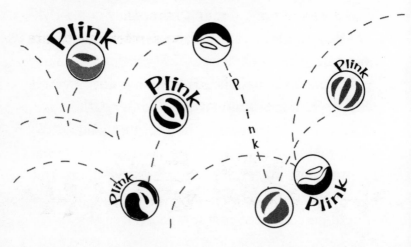

"Stop! Stop them!" shrieked Grant, as his marbles bounced out of control through the halls of the museum. "HELP! I'm losing my marbles!" He scrambled to scoop up the elusive trinkets.

"I see that I'm not the only one *losing his marbles* on this trip," Papa chuckled.

Grant soon returned, unsuccessful in the attempt to reclaim his marbles.

"Stop laughing at me!" Grant shouted, with a red face. "It's not funny!"

"Oh, Grant, we're not really laughing at you," Mimi said.

"Yes, you are!" Grant persisted.

"Grant, the *marbles* I was referring to are statues that were carved out of marble many years ago," Dr. Pothitos said. "I should have explained it more clearly."

The new museum that Mimi, Papa, Christina, and Grant were visiting would eventually be home to all the artifacts from the old, cramped Acropolis museum. It would be a way for people all over the world to experience ancient Greece.

"Can you tell us more about the ancient Greeks?" Christina asked.

"The ancient Greek civilization prospered for about 1,000 years," he said. "At the beginning, they were not a unified country but a loose association of city states like Athens and Sparta. The ancient Greeks gave us the foundations of our democracy, our system of laws, our science, our mathematics, and our music."

"It sounds like the Greeks invented everything," said Christina.

"Almost everything," Dr. Pothitos said with a wink.

"I know something the Greeks *didn't* invent," said Grant, giggling. "Clothes! Look at all these nekkid statues!"

Mimi smiled at Grant's remark. "The Greeks celebrated the perfection of the human body," she explained.

"Oh," Grant said with a shrug.

"Dr. Pothitos, can you tell us more about the invading Turkish army that took over the Parthenon?" asked Christina.

"The Turks from the old Ottoman Empire invaded Greece hundreds of years ago," he said. "The Turkish army captured the Parthenon and were fighting an army from Venice, Italy. During that battle, much of the inside of the Parthenon was destroyed."

"What was inside the Parthenon?" asked Grant.

"Many sculptures inside the Parthenon were damaged," Dr. Pothitos said. "Some of them were destroyed beyond repair."

"Then the Turks let the British people steal them," Melina added.

"They stole them?" exclaimed Christina. "That's not fair."

"The British did not really steal them," Dr. Pothitos said. "The Turks allowed a British nobleman named Thomas Bruce, Earl of Elgin, to bring them to England. A few years later, he sold them to the British Museum in London.

The Elgin Marbles, as they are now called, are still in London."

"They need to be brought back home to the Parthenon," said Alex.

"Let the British keep them," said Grant. "Finders, keepers is what I say."

"I've been working with our government for years to get them back to Greece, their rightful home," said Dr. Pothitos. "I'd like to see them in this very museum."

"I think it's only right that they should be brought back here," Christina said.

Dr. Pothitos spread his arms wide. "Take a look around the museum and enjoy yourselves," he suggested.

Christina and Grant marveled at the ancient sculptures, vases, and other relics.

"What's this?" asked Christina.

"It's the most amazing invention," said Alex. "It's the first known computer. The small box was stuffed with cogs and moving parts. When someone turned a handle, the computer displayed the movements of planets."

"Cool," Grant remarked. "There sure are a lot of statues in here!"

"Which one is that?" asked Christina, looking at the stark white sculpture in front of her.

"That's the god Apollo," said Melina. "You know, the one with the curse!"

Christina shuddered.

"I've seen all the nekkid statues I care to see today," said Grant. "They're giving me the creeps. I feel like they are all staring at me."

"Come on, kids," Papa called in his booming voice. With Christina in the lead, Alex and Melina raced to the exit.

Grant remained at the foot of Apollo's statue. He placed the gold and black amulet in Apollo's marble hand. "Apollo, I know you want this back," Grant said. "Please don't curse any of us, especially not my Papa."

As Grant turned away, a figure shrouded in a black, hooded robe slid out of the shadows. He plucked the amulet from Apollo's hand. *The kids had no idea that someone had been following them through the museum.*

10

When in Plaka...

Mimi, Papa, Christina, and Grant returned to the hotel lobby with Dr. Pothitos and his grandchildren.

"I am sorry we won't be able to go with you to Plaka today," Dr. Pothitos said. "I was really looking forward to celebrating *Apokreas* with you."

"Mimi," Grant said, "what is *Apokreas* again?"

"*Apokreas* is a 40-day period of celebration in Greece," Mimi replied. "People come into town dressed in all sorts of costumes. It's a time of music, dancing, eating, and having fun. It ends just before Easter. I've read all about it and can't wait!" she added.

"It's okay that you can't be with us, Nick," Papa said, giving Dr. Pothitos a big slap on the back. "Like I always say, work before play."

"It's not exactly work," Dr. Pothitos said. "A friend of mine at the Athens Police Department said he had some important information to pass along to me."

"I hope it's not serious, Nick," said Mimi.

"I am not certain, but I fear it has to do with the antiquities at the new museum or the Acropolis," Dr. Pothitos said.

While the adults were busy talking, Grant motioned for Christina, Alex, and Melina to join him in the hotel's Lost and Found closet.

"Did you find another note, Grant?" asked Christina.

"No, it's not a note," Grant replied. "It's something even better. We don't have to worry about the curse anymore."

"Why is that?" asked Christina.

"Let's just say I used some logic, Christina," Grant proudly proclaimed. "I figured the amulet belonged to Apollo. It did have his name on it."

"Go on," said Christina.

"I gave the amulet back to Apollo," he continued. "Now he'll leave us alone since I gave it back to him."

"You are one smart boy," Melina said, as she hugged Grant.

"How did you manage to 'give' it to Apollo?" asked Alex.

"I put it in his hands," said Grant.

"You mean you saw Apollo walking down the street?" asked Melina, with a puzzled look.

"No, he was standing in the museum," said Grant.

"You gave it to a statue," Alex moaned, and rolled his eyes.

"Grant! Christina!" called Mimi. "Where are you?"

"We've got to go now, Grant," Christina said.

The children quickly slipped out of the closet.

"Is there something I can help you kids find?" asked the bellman suspiciously.

"No, we were just playing," Grant answered.

"I suggest you find other places to play," said the bellman, with a scowl. The children didn't know he had heard every word they said in the closet. He slipped away quietly as Papa approached.

"There you are!" Papa bellowed. "You two had better hurry up. We've got to change clothes and get to *Plaka*. We don't want to keep Mimi waiting."

"I can't believe I've got to wear this dress in public," Grant complained, as he walked down the hotel corridor. "I look like a sissy. I hope I don't run into anyone from home."

"I doubt we'll run into anyone from Peachtree City, Georgia," Christina said.

Grant and Christina were dressed in traditional Greek costumes. Mimi wanted to make sure the four of them would be celebrating *Apokreas* in grand style. Grant wore a long-sleeved, white garment that hit just below the knees. It looked like a nightshirt. On top of the white garment, he wore a gold cummerbund, similar to a big, thick belt. His outfit was topped off with a red vest and a red hat, called a *fez*, on his head.

Grant began to giggle uncontrollably as Papa appeared in the hall dressed exactly like him. "I'm not sure what you're laughing at, pardner," Papa said. "Don't you know all fashionable Greeks wear this?" With that said, Papa and Grant leaned against the wall, howling with laughter.

"Look at my two men," Mimi said, smiling. "Why, don't you two look adorable?"

"So, what do you think about me?" Christina said, twirling around so Mimi could see her from all sides.

"You and Mimi aren't dressed much different from Papa and me," said Grant.

Mimi and Christina wore traditional Greek costumes for women, starting with red skirts that touched their feet. They each wore a white blouse with a gold and black vest. The tops of their heads were crowned with something resembling a large black beret with a long gold tassel.

"Do I have to go outside dressed like this?" asked Grant.

"Yes, you do," said Mimi. "And I bet you will have fun, too. In Plaka, everyone will be wearing costumes. There is a lot to learn there, too," she added. "Plaka is in the middle of historic and ancient Athens. It's the oldest continuously occupied part of Athens."

Grant and his family soon found out that they were in the middle of one of the world's biggest parties. *Apokreas* was like New Year's Day, St. Patrick's Day, Halloween, Mardi Gras, and Cinco de Mayo wrapped into one big celebration.

"Hey, take it easy with that," exclaimed Christina, wincing slightly. "What was that?"

"I believe that cute little boy who just bonked you on the head is saying 'hello' or something like that," explained Mimi. "Hitting you over the head with a red plastic bat is how people greet one another during *Apokreas*."

"A simple handshake would be better," Christina said, rubbing her head. "I don't like being smacked on the head with a bat, plastic or not!"

"That didn't hurt, did it, Christina?" asked Grant.

"Not really, it just startled me," she said.

"You'd better get used to it, little lady," Papa remarked. "Mimi says we can expect this to happen a lot when walking these narrow streets of Plaka."

"Look, it's snowing!" squealed Grant.

"That may look like snow, Grant," said Mimi, "but it's really confetti."

Confetti covered the streets and their clothes. The confetti was so thick that Grant was convinced he had been caught in a blizzard.

The streets were alive with musicians, photographers, and people selling flowers and beads. Christina even saw people offering to write her name on a grain of rice.

"It's time we take a break from all this fun and go inside," said Papa.

Mimi spied a souvenir shop just ahead and quickly darted inside, followed by Papa and Christina.

"Look at the beautiful coral, Christina," Mimi said. "Let's take a look around. You know how I like to shop!" She spotted something she thought Grant would like. "Grant, what do you think about this?" Mimi asked, turning to look for him. *"Grant?"*

11

Volcanoes and Calderas

The mysterious hooded figure crept toward Grant. The alley seemed narrower and darker as it approached him. He spotted a silver ring on one of its fingers. Grant tried to run, but his feet felt like lead weights. The figure spoke with a serpent-like hiss, "You will come with me to Santorini. Apollo's Oracle has a message for you."

As the figure was about to snatch Grant's arm, a man dressed like a waiter hit the figure on the head. It fell to its knees from the impact of the hard, red bat.

Grant took advantage of this opportunity to escape and raced to the souvenir shop.

"There you are!" said Mimi, startled to see Grant fly through the shop's door.

"We need to go to Santorini," he said, panting.

"I've heard it's quite a place," Papa remarked. "The island is full of surprises, according to the Greeks."

"Santorini it is!" exclaimed Mimi. "Papa, let's go to the airport once we finish shopping."

"Can I get anything else for you?" asked the flight attendant.

"No, thank you," said Mimi. "This coffee will do just fine."

"I see you want to be wide awake when we get to the island," Papa said with a smile.

The sky began to darken as the sun slipped low over the sparkling blue Aegean Sea.

"Good evening, ladies and gentlemen. This is your captain speaking," said the pilot. "In approximately twenty minutes, we will be landing at Santorini."

Christina sat motionless in her seat. Why did someone want to grab Grant? Would they run into Apollo's Oracle? Was there really a 'friend' trying to help? Christina was glad that Alex, Melina, and their grandfather were with them on this trip to Santorini.

The airplane finally landed on the island. Everyone was quickly whisked away by George, the taxicab driver. "You'll love it here on Santorini," said George, as the taxi inched its way up the dark road. "The view from the hotel in the morning is spectacular."

"I can hardly wait for morning," said Mimi. The taxi sped away into the night, as the seven weary travelers checked into the hotel and settled into their beds.

"You can open your eyes now," said Mimi.

"WOW!"

howled Grant in excitement.

"THAT'S INCREDIBLE!"

shouted Christina, flabbergasted.

"I nearly jumped out of my skin the first time Grandpa Pothitos brought us here," said Alex.

"Me, too," Melina added.

"Look at those toy ships down there!" exclaimed Grant.

Christina and Grant stood at the outside edge of a giant volcano. Two thousand feet below, Grant watched giant merchant ships steaming out to sea. The massive tankers looked like tiny model boats.

"What's the ocean doing way up here?" exclaimed Grant, as he turned around to look at the center of the volcano.

"What you see, Grant, is the volcano's caldera," said Dr. Pothitos. "Many hundreds of years ago, this volcano erupted. After the eruption, the volcano caved in on itself. Over a span of several hundred years, water filled the crater, and that's what you are now looking at."

"Will the volcano ever erupt again?" asked Christina.

"It is a live volcano, so it will very likely erupt again," said Dr. Pothitos.

"Then we better get off this thing!" exclaimed Grant.

"Don't worry, Grant," Dr. Pothitos reassured him. "It won't erupt any time soon."

"Kids, be careful out here," said Mimi. "Don't get too close to the edge of the cliff. We're going to walk back to the hotel."

"We'll be careful," said Christina, "and I'll watch out for Grant."

"I can watch out for myself," Grant protested.

Dr. Pothitos, Mimi, and Papa slowly disappeared as they hiked back to the hotel.

"Here's what happened yesterday," said Christina, as the other three kids huddled around her. "Grant was messing with those funny Greek shoes and when he looked up, there was someone in a black hood trying to grab him. Then a man dressed like a waiter clobbered the guy in the hood with a bat, and Grant escaped."

"The guy was going to bring me here to meet Apollo's Oracle," said Grant. He let out a sigh. "I'm getting really tired of thinking about it. Hey, look over there, Alex. I'll race you to that tree!"

The two boys dashed toward an olive grove. "No one can catch the mighty Hercules!" Grant shouted.

Alex chased Grant as fast as his legs would carry him. Melina yanked Christina's arm to get her to join in on the chase. Christina reluctantly followed.

"Can't catch me," Grant squealed as he wove his way through the thick mass of olive trees.

"CAN CATCH YOU"

an ominous voice cried out.

The frightening figure in a billowing black robe loomed in front of Grant. He stopped abruptly, shivering at the sight before him.

"You have been warned, mortal," the figure moaned in an unearthly tone. *"Heed these words. Apollo speaks. Do not disturb the Acropolis. A curse will haunt those who trespass."*

12

The Phantom of the Olive Grove

Goosebumps ran down Christina's back as the hooded figure vanished from sight. "What was that, Grant?" asked Christina. She had only caught a glimpse of the shadowy figure.

"I...tsssss.........ah...ah...ah...gaa...gaa...ghost," Grant stuttered. "It...ah...ah...pa...peared from nowhere and then just dis...ah...pa...pa...peared!"

"This is getting really spooky." Christina said.

"I n-n-n-know," stuttered Grant. "Le...le...let's...get out of here!"

Grant described the sight he had seen to Christina. She reviewed the clues they had found so far as they stumbled out of the mysterious olive grove. This was their list of clues: Christina's dream, Grant's amulet, Papa losing control of the *Mystery Girl* and himself, the strange motorcycle accident, the note from the "friendly" waiter, the silver, skull-shaped pinkie rings and the people wearing them, the hooded figure, and now, this phantom!

"Grant, what do these clues have in common and why would that waiter refer to us as 'friends'?" asked Christina. Mimi had always told Christina to use her grey matter when solving a mystery, and Christina was attempting to eliminate any red herrings. She was determined to get to the bottom of this *Curse of the Acropolis*. Grant didn't answer. He stared into space with a blank expression on his face.

Mimi, Papa, and Dr. Pothitos relaxed at the hotel, sipping coffee in the crowded café. "What did your detective friend at the police department have to say, Nick?" asked Mimi.

"He said they are on the trail of an international smuggling ring," explained Dr. Pothitos. "The police have been getting help from one of the ring's members. He has been sending notes anonymously. This ring of thieves steals priceless treasures from museums around the world. My detective friend fears the criminals will strike at our new museum. I told my colleagues to be especially cautious of strangers appearing at our dig. Dr. Mendilos seemed especially interested in this ring of thieves. He wanted to know all the details that the police had on the crime ring."

"Who is Dr. Mendilos?" asked Mimi.

"Dr. Mendilos is the most brilliant archaeologist I have ever met," Dr. Pothitos replied. "As a matter of fact, he taught me everything I know about ancient Greece and is the main reason I decided to become an archaeologist. *He* is the one who should be leading my expedition. I am humbled to have him on my team."

"We're tickled *you* asked us to be part of your team's first dig at the Acropolis," Papa said.

"I'm glad I invited you to come along on the dig," Dr. Pothitos replied. "With all the **tedious** work I have to do at the Acropolis, I doubt I could keep track of people attempting to steal artifacts. I know I can count on you two to be on the lookout for thieves."

"Christina and Grant will be your biggest help," Mimi said. "You know how inquisitive children are."

Mimi glanced at her watch with a worried look. The kids had been gone a long time and she was getting worried about them. Just as Mimi and Papa were about to leave to look for them, the four kids burst through the café's entrance.

"Why, Grant, you look like you've seen a ghost!" exclaimed Mimi. Grant was shaking.

A Speeding Ferry Boat

"Wait for Papa, wait!" Grant cried at the top of his lungs. Grant thought for sure that Papa would be left behind on the volcano. The boat was shoving off, waiting for no one. Papa leaped from the pier just in time.

"Perfect landing!" Papa shouted, proud of his excellent timing.

"What do you say we rustle up some chow, Grant?" said Papa, ruffling Grant's blond hair.

"Do you suppose they'll have some of that really good soufflé stuff on this ferry?" asked Grant.

"You mean *souvlaki,* Grant?" asked Alex.

"Soufflé, *souvlaki,* it's all Greek to me," said Grant, giggling.

"Grant, if I hear that one more time...," said Christina, gritting her teeth.

"This looks like the place," interrupted Grant, as the hungry group shuffled into the ship's snack bar.

"I'm sorry we don't have a very large selection of things to eat," the waiter said. "But I'm sure you'll like what we do have."

"I'll take that sandwich, please," said Grant.

"Let me heat that for you, young man," the waiter offered. "Please, have a seat and relax. I'll bring the food to your table."

"Did you notice, Melina," whispered Alex, "that's the same waiter that passed Grant the note. I wonder why he's following us."

"He even has on that same silver skull ring on his pinkie finger," said Melina.

"He sure seems to be *acting* friendly," said Grant. "A bit *too* friendly."

"What are all of you kids whispering about?" asked Mimi.

"Nothing, Mimi," said Christina.

"You kids sure seem to be acting like there is a secret," said Mimi.

The waiter and his helper came to the table with their arms full of white china plates.

"Here you go," said the waiter. "Lunch is served. Enjoy!"

As Grant bit into his sandwich, he discovered a surprise—a piece of paper! "Christina," Grant whispered, "I think our 'friend' left me another note! This time he put it in my sandwich."

"What does it say?" asked Christina.

"Let's look at it in private with Alex and Melina," Grant suggested.

After they finished eating lunch, the group left the snack bar to look around the ship. The modern Superferry was filled with rows of comfortable seats, tables, TVs, and game rooms.

"We'll meet up with you later, Mimi," said Christina. "You know where to find us."

Christina knew that Mimi would know to look for them in the game room. Grant led the kids to a secluded corner to read the note.

"Let me read it," Alex said. He grabbed the note and his eyes grew wide.

"Why is he calling us his friends?" Christina asked. "Maybe, just maybe what he's saying is true. He is actually afraid we might get hurt."

"But he's wearing that same ring all the other creepy guys are wearing," said Alex.

"I still think he's trying to trick us into believing he is our friend because he wants something," said Melina.

"I'm not sure, but I think he is our friend," said Christina. "Something about him is different."

"Next stop—Athens!" Papa called out in his booming voice, summoning the kids from the game room.

Olympics and Cavemen

"Look how strong the mighty Zeus is," exclaimed Grant, as he lugged a duffel bag in each hand along with a bulging backpack on his back. The Superferry had just pulled in from its five-hour cruise from Santorini. Grant looked like a walking luggage rack. He had volunteered to carry Melina's and Mimi's overnight bags in addition to his own bag. From the ferry, they would take a taxi to Philopappou Hill.

"I thought Zeus was the guy who threw lightning bolts," Christina said, smiling.

"Zeus, Hercules, it's all....." Grant began.

"We know, 'it's all Greek to me,'" Mimi, Papa, and Christina said, interrupting Grant before he could finish.

Grant's face was beaming. He had lugged all those bags by himself and hadn't tripped once all the way from the ferry to the taxicab. He didn't even have to stop for a rest. "I'm the Olympic champion of bag carrying," he boasted, dropping the bags to the curb with a thud.

Papa held up his hand, hoping to get a taxi driver's attention.

"Speaking of Olympics, Grant, did you know that the Olympics were invented by the Greeks?" explained Dr. Pothitos. "In ancient Greece, the Olympic games were held to honor Zeus. The games were part of a great five-day festival held every four years at Olympia, a valley near a city called Elis."

"Did other nations come to the first Olympics?" asked Christina.

"The first Olympics were only for Greeks," Dr. Pothitos replied. "The early Greeks,

however, did not a have a single nation called Greece. Cities like Athens and Sparta had their own governments, and there were often wars between the cities. Messengers sent out from Elis announced a sacred truce of one month before the festival began. The truce meant that people could travel to Olympia in safety. The Olympic games were more important than wars because they were a religious festival."

"What kind of events did they have at the first Olympics?" Grant asked.

"In those days," Dr. Pothitos explained, "the only event was a short sprint, from one end of the stadium to the other. Gradually, more events were added over the years until there were four days of many different competitions."

"I would have won the gold medal in the first Olympics," claimed Grant, bending his skinny arm to show off his bicep muscle.

"I bet you would have, my man," Papa said.

"In the ancient Olympic games, they didn't give medals to the winners," said Dr. Pothitos.

"No medals?" Grant said, frowning.

"Then what did the winners get?" asked Christina.

"They got to wear a crown of olive leaves," said Dr. Pothitos.

"What a rip-off!" exclaimed Grant.

"They got more than just that," said Dr. Pothitos. "Successful athletes enjoyed great benefits from their home city for the rest of their lives. They received free meals, invitations to banquets, and specially reserved seats in the theatre."

Papa glanced at the sky. "From the looks of things up there, Zeus might start unleashing some lightning bolts pretty soon," he remarked. "Let's get in these 'specially reserved' taxicabs."

The shiny yellow taxis sped away from the harbor but began to labor up the hill. At Philopappou Hill's summit, Grant and Christina were treated to a spectacular view of the Acropolis.

"A great Greek general once built a fort here to help protect Athens," said Dr. Pothitos. "Later, a Roman governor, named Philopappou, tore the fort down and built a monument in its place. That is why this is called Philopappou Hill.

"The Romans captured and influenced much of the world," Dr. Pothitos continued. "In fact, Grant's hero Hercules was called Herakles before the Romans changed his name."

"The Romans took over Greece?" asked Christina. "That doesn't sound fair."

"You sound like the Greek philosopher Socrates," said Dr. Pothitos. "He too had a good sense of what was fair and not fair."

Socrates was the real reason Dr. Pothitos had brought them to Philopappou Hill. Tucked away in the corner of the hill were several caves with bars across their entrances. One of them was the cell where Socrates was jailed.

"Our famous philosopher, Socrates, was held in this very prison over 2,000 years ago," said Dr. Pothitos, as he led the group to the dark, dreary caves carved out of a massive rock wall. "His crime was nothing more than thinking differently from others in his time, and his ultimate punishment was death."

Mimi, Papa, and the children stared silently at the eerie caverns. "So, how would you like to spend your last days in there?" Dr. Pothitos asked.

"No way!" Grant shouted.

"I can't even imagine spending one night in there, much less months and years," Mimi said, shuddering.

"I guess you wouldn't get room service there with *baklava* on your morning breakfast tray, would you, Mimi?" Papa teased.

Mimi straightened her bright red baseball cap. "I'm not that spoiled, am I?" she asked with a smile. She grabbed Papa's elbow. "Let's look around a little more before it rains," she said, leading Papa and Dr. Pothitos down a gravel path.

A True Friend?

The children stayed behind, fascinated by the cave prison. Alex and Grant wrapped their fingers around the rough iron bars across one of the cave entrances. "Do you think I can get in there?" Grant asked Alex with a mischievous glint in his eye.

"I dare you to try it," Alex said.

Grant turned sideways, sliding his right leg and hip through the bars. They fit! He grinned at Alex. "I'll take your dare," he said.

With little more than a wiggle or two, Grant slipped into the cave where Socrates had been imprisoned centuries before. It smelled old and wet. He ran his fingers along the rocky wall and shuffled his feet across the dusty floor. He looked back at the entrance, glad to see Alex's smiling face peering between the bars.

"You did it!" Alex cried. "What's it like in there?"

"Grant!" Christina's voice echoed around the cave walls. "What are you doing in there?" She and Melina had been talking, not noticing what the boys were up to.

"Checking things out," Grant said. "I think I see some bat poop in here."

"Oh, Grant," Christina said. "You'd better get out of there before Mimi and Papa come back here."

Just then, Papa's booming voice made her jump.

"Kids!" he shouted. "It's time to go! It's going to start pouring any minute and I don't like getting caught in a Greek thunderstorm any more than an American one!"

"Okay, Papa!" Christina called. She stuck her face in between the bars. "You get out of there right now, little brother!"

"I'm coming," Grant replied.

A crash of thunder and a flash of lightning startled the kids. "Let's go!" shouted Melina. She grabbed Christina and started running up the hill toward the adults. Alex was right behind them. They had forgotten about Grant in their hurry to escape the storm.

Just as Grant was slipping back through the bars, lightning illuminated the prison cell. Something near the back wall caught his eye. Maybe it's something cool to take as a souvenir, he thought. He shuffled back to the wall in the darkness and felt around with his hand. His fingers stopped on a folded sheet of paper.

"Don't lose that," a voice whispered.

Grant whirled around. "Who are you?" he said, shivering with fright. "Where are you?"

There was no answer. Grant squinted his eyes, trying to see anything, but the cell was black. He scrambled through the bars, tearing the back pocket of his shorts. Hard pellets of rain began to fall, soaking him to the skin as he raced up the path after his family and friends.

"Grant, is that you—finally?" Christina called.

"I fa...fa...found this note in the cave," Grant said, breathing heavily from fear and fatigue. "A scary voice told me not to lose it, and I didn't."

"What does it say?" Melina asked, as Alex took the soggy note from Grant's hand.

Beware of the one they call The Phantom.

Your friend.

Meteora

"It's a shame Dr. Pothitos can't join us today," said Mimi. "He would have made the perfect tour guide."

"He's a good friend to fill in for Dr. Mendilos at the last minute," said Papa.

"I'm glad he allowed Alex and Melina to stay with us today," Mimi added, smiling at how the kids were chattering together in the back of the bus.

The bus strained as it crept up the steep and craggy cliffs. "Ladies and gentlemen, behold Meteora," said Phillip, the bus driver. "*Meteora* in Greek means suspended rocks. The sandstone towers here were first used as a religious retreat when a hermit named Barnabas lived in one of its caves more than 1,000 years ago."

"What's a religious retreat, Mimi?" asked Grant, looking puzzled.

"It's a place where people go to get away from the rest of the world, or society, and just think about God and other religious things," explained Mimi. "A religious retreat is also called a monastery."

Christina marveled at the spectacular sight. Like massive skyscrapers, Meteora's giant sandstone towers stretched to the heavens. Perched on these rocky peaks were more than 20 different monasteries built over a period of several hundred years.

"Whooaa," exclaimed Grant. "I hope they have an elevator to the top of that one." He was pointing at the Moni Rousanou monastery. It sat at the very tip of a narrow spire of rock. "My neck hurts looking up at it," he said, blinking in the bright sun.

"How do we get up to the monasteries?" asked Christina.

"In the 1920s, stairs were cut into the rock making it easier to climb up there," said Phillip.

"How did they get those buildings to the top?" asked Grant.

"We're not certain how the first people got to the top of these steep rocks," explained Phillip. "One popular theory is that kites were flown over the tops, carrying strings attached to thicker ropes, which were made into the first rope ladders."

"Rope ladders!" exclaimed Grant. "It must have been like boarding a huge pirate ship!"

"I'll bet when we get up there," Alex remarked, "the wind will be blowing in our faces like we're really on a pirate ship!" He and Grant grinned at each other in anticipation.

"Enjoy your visit to the monasteries here at Meteora," said Phillip. "The bus will be waiting right here for you when you are finished exploring."

"Those things look scary," said Melina, as the group started up the stairs. She was afraid the monasteries could come toppling down at any moment.

"Don't be scared," said Alex, reassuring her. "People have lived up here in the monasteries for hundreds of years. There are even monks and nuns living in some of them today."

"Yeah, but don't look down, either," said Christina, stepping cautiously as they crossed a bridge connecting two huge spires.

"I'll bet we are more than 1,000 feet high," Papa said in amazement. "And we've got a few hundred more feet to go to reach the top."

"Don't remind me," said Mimi, as she crossed the bridge.

"Last one to the top is a rotten egg," screeched Grant, as he raced up the stairs.

In an instant, or so it seemed, Grant was at the top of the steep hill. He really did feel like a pirate. He imagined himself perched in the crow's nest, at the top of a tall sailing ship's giant mast.

Christina had tried to keep up with Grant, but he quickly disappeared into the monastery. Alex and Melina plodded up the steps along with Mimi and Papa.

It sure seems lonely in this old church, Grant thought. He decided to turn back to find the others, but it was easy to get lost in the empty monastery with its maze of courtyards and buildings. Instead of retracing his steps through the abbey, Grant wandered through an arch that led him to a different and more chilling monastery.

Christina's voice echoed in the empty church. "Grant, where are you?"

"Go back to your home now and never return to Greece!" a voice shrieked.

Christina was shocked. The sound was hideous, and it spoke in a tone that sounded strangely familiar to her. Christina turned around and didn't see anyone in any direction.

Alex and Melina entered the old sanctuary, followed closely by Mimi and Papa.

"Did you ever catch up to him?" asked Melina.

"No, I didn't, and I can't seem to find him anywhere," said Christina.

"I'm sure we'll find Grant somewhere around here," said Papa. "He couldn't have gone too far."

As they searched the monastery for Grant, Christina told Alex and Melina about the haunting voice she had just heard and what she was planning to do.

"So, you've figured this out, Christina?" asked Melina.

"I'm almost certain," Christina replied, "but I need a little help from Alex."

Just then Mimi and Papa appeared with Grant in tow. Grant looked pale and shaken as he stumbled behind Papa. *Once again, he had encountered the Phantom of the Olive Grove.*

17

Acropolis by Moonlight

Mimi, Papa, and the children gathered around Dr. Pothitos. His team had arrived about an hour earlier to prepare the site for this evening's historic dig at the Acropolis.

"This is perfect weather," said Dr. Pothitos, grinning from ear to ear. "Not a cloud in the sky and a full moon. You kids are in for a real treat. They are starting the light show—the entire Acropolis is about to be bathed in magnificent colors!"

The full moon added a golden glow to the night sky as the Acropolis changed from white to blue, then red, then a multitude of changing colors.

"Christina," Melina whispered, "it's not too late for us to warn Grandpa Pothitos of the curse. I'm scared."

"Don't be scared, Melina," Christina said. "Remember, I have a plan." Melina thought Christina was being **obstinate**. She didn't understand why they were ignoring Apollo's curse and the oracle.

As the light show ended, Dr. Pothitos gathered his team and went over their plan for the evening.

"I'm so pleased you were able to make it, Dr. Mendilos," said Dr. Pothitos, shaking his hand. "I'm glad to hear your family emergency turned out to be a false alarm."

Dr. Mendilos had a sly grin on his face. "So am I," he remarked. "I wouldn't have missed this dig for the world."

"I knew it," Christina said softly to herself. Dr. Mendilos had a silver ring in the shape of a skull on his pinkie finger. Alex and Christina grinned at one another.

"This is exciting, being a part of your team's historic first dig at the Acropolis," said Mimi.

"What can I do to help?" asked Grant.

Dr. Pothitos assigned each of the kids a different task. Alex and Grant would dig, Melina would dust the artifacts, and Christina would wrap and catalog them.

The team labored for several hours. Grant enjoyed digging for the buried treasure. He felt like he was a Greek pirate. Grant thought that Alex must not like digging for treasure as much as he did, since Alex left to run an errand barely after he started. What could be more exciting than this, Grant wondered.

Most of the items the team found were old trinkets. Every once in a while, they discovered an antiquity worth keeping. Dr. Pothitos was pleased with the artifacts they discovered. He even felt that some of them would end up in the new museum.

As the team was wrapping up their work for the evening, Dr. Pothitos was startled to see Dr. Mendilos charging at him with a police officer at his heels. He stood up to face them and noticed two artifacts sticking out of his jacket pockets as he brushed the dirt off his clothes.

"How did these get here?" he asked in amazement.

"Arrest him, Officer!" said Dr. Mendilos, pointing his finger.

"Take off your jacket sir," said the police officer. Dr. Pothitos removed his jacket, with a look of concern on his face. The police officer pulled the two artifacts from the pockets.

"He's probably behind that crime ring, too," said Dr. Mendilos. His voice was angry and accusing.

"I'm sorry, but I have to do this," said the officer, as he placed the handcuffs on Dr. Pothitos.

"Wait just a minute!" Dr. Pothitos protested. "I'm not sure how those got into my pockets, but I can assure you, I am no criminal!"

As the handcuffs snapped into place, Alex ran up with his grandfather's detective friend.

"Hang on, you've got the wrong one!" the detective shouted. "Dr. Mendilos is the one we want."

"What, me?" Dr. Mendilos exclaimed. "What proof do you have?"

"Plenty, thanks to this little lady," said the detective, pointing at Christina. "Dr. Mendilos, we know that you are the leader of an international ring of thieves. You steal from museums around the world and were attempting to steal treasures from the Acropolis. Your crime ring is called The Brotherhood, and you all wear a signature silver skull on your pinkie finger.

"You try to frighten or harm people who stand in your way," the detective continued. "We have evidence that your people disabled a motorcycle, and maybe even a small plane. One of your former members, Christina's *friend*, is willing to testify against you in court."

"I have a question for Dr. Mendilos," asked Dr. Pothitos, with a sad look. "Why did you do this? You were a good man."

"You were stealing my fame!" shouted Dr. Mendilos, his face red with fury. "I wanted you in jail so I could lead the team! It would be easy for me to steal artifacts with you out of the picture."

"How did you figure all of this out, Christina?" asked Mimi proudly.

"It was obvious that he was the culprit," Christina explained, "because every time the Phantom showed up, Dr. Mendilos was missing. I noticed the Phantom's voice sounded like one of our motorcycle drivers, Dr. Mendilos. The Phantom and his gang members—the ones wearing the silver skull ring—have been following us and trying to scare us away from this dig ever since we left that last airport in the *Mystery Girl*."

Christina pointed at Alex. "When the time was right, I sent Alex to get our waiter friend— the one leaving notes warning us to be careful. The waiter said I was right about Dr. Mendilos. He and Alex went straight to Dr. Pothitos' detective friend."

"You have my gratitude," said Dr. Pothitos. He took Christina's hand and kissed it.

"Your face is red, Christina," Grant said, giggling. Christina glared at him, then looked back at Dr. Pothitos. "Thank you," she said.

18

Coincidence?

"Oh! I have slipped the surly bonds of earth..." Papa said, roaring with laughter as the *Mystery Girl* departed Athens. "What—no one's going to stop me this time?"

"I think we'll let you finish, Papa," giggled Christina. "The last time we interrupted you, strange things happened."

"Purely *coincidence*," Papa remarked.

"My head is still swimming from all the clues and people involved from our latest mystery, Christina," said Mimi. "I'm amazed. How did you keep up with all of it?"

"It wasn't easy," confessed Christina. "I had a lot of help from Grant, Alex and Melina. And

it was *no* coincidence that Dr. Mendilos called himself the Phantom."

"And I have plenty of material for my new mystery book," chuckled Mimi. "That *may* be a coincidence."

"I wonder if Apollo kept the amulet I gave him?" asked Grant. "And I wonder if Papa's curse is broken?"

"Apollo must have cancelled the curse, because after you gave Apollo his amulet, Papa hasn't tripped or lost control of himself," giggled Christina. "Do you think that's a *coincidence*?"

Mimi and Papa smiled, knowing that Papa had been losing his balance during their Greek adventure due to an inner ear infection. "Maybe Apollo made you feel better," Mimi whispered.

"All I know is it's ALL GREEK TO ME!" Grant said with a smile.

THE END

About the Author

Carole Marsh is an author and publisher who has written many works of fiction and non-fiction for young readers. She travels throughout the United States and around the world to research her books. In 1979 Carole Marsh was named Communicator of the Year for her corporate communications work with major national and international corporations.

Marsh is the founder and CEO of Gallopade International, established in 1979. Today, Gallopade International is widely recognized as a leading source of educational materials for every state and many countries. Marsh and Gallopade were recipients of the 2004 Teachers' Choice Award. Marsh has written more than 50 Carole Marsh Mysteries™. In 2007, she was named Georgia Author of the year. Years ago, her children, Michele and Michael, were the original characters in her mystery books. Today, they continue the Carole Marsh Books tradition by working at Gallopade. By adding grandchildren Grant and Christina as new mystery characters, she has continued the tradition for a third generation.

Ms. Marsh welcomes correspondence from her readers. You can e-mail her at fanclub@gallopade.com, visit carolemarshmysteries.com, or write to her in care of Gallopade International, P.O. Box 2779, Peachtree City, Georgia, 30269 USA.

Built-In Book Club

Talk About It!

1. The Americans ate some interesting food when visiting Greece. What is the strangest food you've ever eaten?

2. Have you ever visited another country? If so, where did you go? What did you think of it?

3. Hitting someone on the head with a red bat is an unusual greeting. What other ways do people say 'hello' without speaking?

4. Socrates was put in a small, scary prison just for thinking differently! Do you think it's important to speak your mind?

5. Have you ever been to a museum? If so, what was it like? If not, do you think you'd like to visit one someday?

6. Christina had a nightmare that she thought was coming true. Have you ever had an eerie dream like that?

7. In the story, Papa was having a bad time dropping and tripping! Can you remember a day when nothing seemed to work right for you?

8. Grant liked pretending he was a Greek hero. Who do you like to pretend to be?

9. Zeus could throw lightning bolts! What kind of weather would you like to be able to control?

10. Why do you think pieces of ancient art are so highly desired by so many people?

Built-In Book Club

Bring it to Life!

1.   Find a list of the mythical Greek gods. Choose your favorite, and pretend you are one of them. Write a story about what your life is like as a god.

2.   Ask a volunteer to create a 'Note Mystery' like the one Grant had to solve! Leave notes leading to other notes that contain clues about the mystery. Put the notes around the classroom.   Divide into teams to solve the mystery.

3.   Have a pretend Olympics with your class! Come up with fun, creative events like

hula-hooping and jumping on one foot! Crown each champion with a ring of leaves like they did in ancient Greece!

4. Let's play a museum game! Divide the class into three groups: statues, tour guides, and visitors. Students who are statues should strike interesting poses while the tour guides make up interesting stories about them. The visitors should be sure to ask questions and make conversation with the tour guides. When your tour is over, switch groups and play again!

GREECE TRIVIA

1. The country of Greece includes more than 1,000 islands in the Aegean Sea and Ionian Sea.

2. Athens is the name of the capital city of Greece.

3. The Olympics were invented by the ancient Greeks as a way to honor the god Zeus.

4. The Acropolis was built on the top of a hill so that the people living in ancient Athens could better defend themselves.

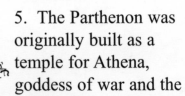

5. The Parthenon was originally built as a temple for Athena, goddess of war and the patron goddess of the city of Athens.

6. When it first began, Greece was not a full country but a union of city-states. Athens and Sparta were two of these city-states.

7. Much of the Parthenon was destroyed during a battle between the Turks and Venetians in 1688.

8. The Elgin Marbles, originally part of the Parthenon, are now in a museum in London, England after the Turks sold them to the British.

9. Apokreas is a 40-day Greek celebration leading up to Easter.

10. The oldest continuously occupied part of Athens is Plaka. It is an old, historic neighborhood with many museums, shops, and restaurants.

Glossary

amulet: a charm worn as protection from evil or to bring good fortune

antiquity: something remaining from ancient times

archaeologist: a person who studies ancient history

buffet: a meal laid out on a long table so that guests may serve themselves

cordial: friendly and sincere

elusive: something that is hard to express or define

mythology: a collection of myths or stories from a certain culture

Glossary

obstinate: stubborn; resistant to guidance or discipline

ominous: threatening evil or harm

oracle: person who brings a message on behalf of a god

resolute: set in purpose or opinion

tedious: long and tiresome

turbulence: unusual gusts and lulls in the wind

Scavenger Hunt

Want to have some fun? Let's go on a scavenger hunt! See if you can find the items below related to the mystery. *(Teachers: you have permission to reproduce this page.)*

1. ___ a video game

2. ___ a ring

3. ___ a marble

4. ___ a kite

5. ___ a toy motorcycle

6. ___ a picture of a Greek statue

7. ___ a baseball

8. ___ something made of red plastic

9. ___ a sandwich

10. ___ a picture of someone wearing a fez

Pop Quiz

1. Where did Zeus live, according to Greek mythology?

2. How do you say 'hello' in Greek?

3. What did the motorcycle gang crash into as they lost control?

4. Where did the baseball that Alex gave to Grant come from?

5. Christina dreamed of an oracle of which Greek god?

6. Who gave the amulet to Grant?

7. What did the priceless marble look like while being transported to the museum?

8. What was the name of the band of thieves stealing priceless artifacts?

Visit the <u>www.carolemarshmysteries.com</u>
website to:

• Join the Carole Marsh Mysteries Fan Club!

• Write a letter to Christina, Grant, Mimi, or Papa!

• Cast your vote for where the next mystery should take place!

• Find fascinating facts about the countries where the mysteries take place!

• Track your reading on an international map!

• Take the Fact or Fiction online quiz!

• Play the Around-the-World Scavenger Hunt computer game!

• Find out where the *Mystery Girl* is flying next!